EENY, MEENY, MINEY, MO and FLO!

by Laurel Molk

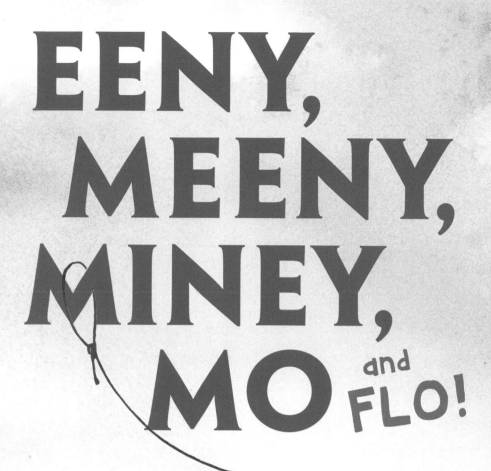

VIKING
An Imprint of Penguin Group (USA)

VIKING

Published by the Penguin Group

Penguin Group (USA) LLC

375 Hudson Street

New York, New York 10014

USA * Canada * UK * Ireland * Australia
New Zealand * India * South Africa * China

penguin.com

A Penguin Random House Company

First published in the United States of America by Viking,
an imprint of Penguin Young Readers Group, 2015

Copyright © 2015 by Laurel Molk

LIBRARY OF CONGRESS CATALOGING-IN-PUBLICATION DATA

Molk, Laurel, author.

Eeny, Meeny, Miney, Mo, and Flo! / by Laurel Molk.

pages cm

Summary: Based on a classic nursery rhyme, four mice brothers attempt to catch animals, only to lose
track of their sister, Flo, in the process.

ISBN 978-0-670-01538-2

1. Mice—Juvenile fiction. 2. Brothers and sisters—Juvenile fiction. 3. Stories in rhyme.
[1. Stories in rhyme. 2. Mice—Fiction. 3. Brothers and sisters—Fiction.] I. Title.

PZ8.3.M7194Ee 2015

[E]—dc23

2014028531

Manufactured in China

1 3 5 7 9 10 8 6 4 2

Set in Cosmiqua Com   Book design by Eileen Savage

The paintings for this book were rendered in watercolor and pen and ink,
and combined digitally using Adobe Photoshop.

To PMM and JAM

Eeny,   Meeny,

Miney, Mo.

Catch a **TIGER** by the toe.

You have to go.

You're too little.

If he **HOLLERS**, let him go.

Eeny, Meeny, Miney, Mo.

Eeny, Meeny, Miney, Mo.

Catch a **HIPPO** by the toe.

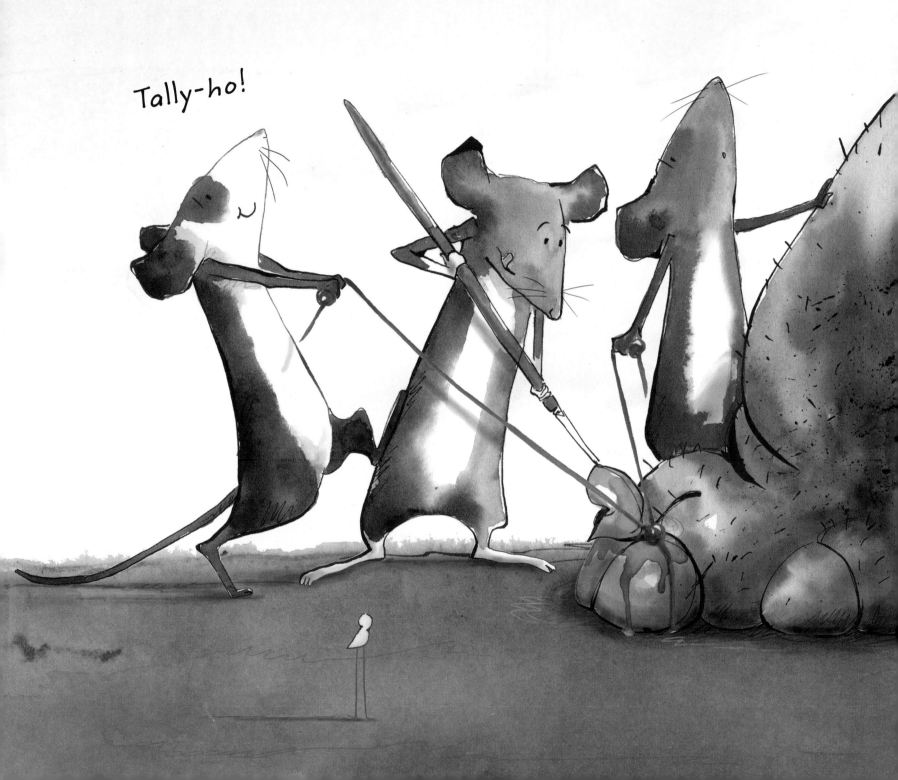

If she **SNEEZES**, let her go.

Eeny, Meeny, Miney, Mo.

Catch a **BOA** by the toe.

Flo, we said no.

If he **SLITHERS**, let him go.

Um, I think he's slithering.

Catch a **TURTLE** by the . . .

Yawn.

Catch a **DODO** by the toe.

Eeny, Meeny, Miney, Mo.

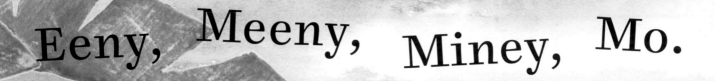

Eeny, Meeny, Miney, Mo.

Hey, isn't that Flo's scarf?

OH NO!

Where'd she go?

Catch a **GATOR** by the toe.

Eeny, Meeny, Miney, Mo...